AF350055

SERMONS OF LOVE

BY

ARYAN DASH

pencil

ISBN 978-93-5438-888-0
© Aryan Dash 2021
Published in India 2021 by Pencil

A brand of
One Point Six Technologies Pvt. Ltd.
123, Building J2, Shram Seva Premises,
Wadala Truck Terminal, Wadala (E)
Mumbai 400037, Maharashtra, INDIA
E connect@thepencilapp.com
W www.thepencilapp.com

All rights reserved worldwide

No part of this publication may be reproduced, stored in or introduced into a retrieval system, or transmitted, in any form, or by any means (electronic, mechanical, photocopying, recording or otherwise), without the prior written permission of the Publisher. Any person who commits an unauthorized act in relation to this publication can be liable to criminal prosecution and civil claims for damages.

DISCLAIMER: *The opinions expressed in this book are those of the authors and do not purport to reflect the views of the Publisher.*

Author biography

Just another teen to the world full of random ones but a conssioueur of literature. I am 18 and in school but love to write poetries and musings. I blog sometimes and mostly read all sorts of books from murder mysteries to magical realism. I've been writing for a year or more now kindling as my book says with Poetry.

Acknowledgements

"TO WHOMEVER I HAVE LOVED."

Introduction

Sermons Of Love a month long work on proses and poetry of experiences with love and thoughts about it. Filled with proses of heartbreak to finding love. The warmth of that first love to agonising heartbreaks and unsuccessful love stories the musings try to cover my thoughts upon it as I penned down the feelings straight from my heart.

Contents

Insomnia Of Love

The notion of love is so powerful it can fill the somber mood of an afternoon like thorny deserts of Sahara with the most exquisite aroma of roses like they have been planted by God himself welcoming into the land of love where is brewed the potions of love that drives you mad in the agony of your failed lover from an age that glorifies love like those in books and poetries but is a mere illusion which the hopeless lovers seem to be looking for dragging feets drenched in the beliefs of finding true love but getting stabs of betrayal everytime they cross paths with someone inconsiderate of being a lover. Oh! How I remember being one of these hapless lovers searching for meaning of love in vague words of my ever lying accomplice to whom I pledged all my enduring love filled with fits of passion enraged in the warm fires of my memory but that was all drowsed by tears of pain over getting bereft of the hand that held me in need but now I'm left with long memories of hers etched in blank pages of my heart. I've become an insomniac lover of the past who avoids sleep to not come across the face of his long gone sweetheart.

In Search Of Warmth

Once a man looned by the absence of love wandered across seven seas in search of alms in the arms of some, seeking the warmth of soul not mere body. He sought peace in love but the world left him alone to struggle. His journey so remarkable kept walking miles staying in the buildings having caught time's rust. Never complained this man predestined whose fate but unshattering his faith who would walk into the doors of heaven if not he could find the warmth he sought in the arms of dream's woman. Knocked on doors, slept on floors and wept on his own years of struggle salvaged nothing but boredom of lonesome. The memoir of his journey calligraphed into a diary his companion in misery who kept a check on the state of his lunacy. To the man who knew nothing but the extent he would keep walking looking for love, looking for shelter in someone's heartbeat his journey so astounding the man's hunt forwarmness.

FOUND YOU

The fateful night of season belonging to monsoon so dark that the roads were illuminated only by the guiding stars. The streets so empty, people on roads straying or laying down accepting the cruel realities of life felt so obsolete to me. Some drowned in the sewers of intoxication while some lost in hazy thoughts of survival when the rain stops, sun rises, a new day begins and with it a new struggle as well to feed one's belly. Just when I was feeling all hopeless, lost in the very city of dreams that had for so many years borne the brunts of people like me in search of our destinies, my eyes fell on some mirage for the beauty amidst such grim people and such impertinent night was surreal, unfathomable as well to have found you. The guide and friend to my infinite sufferings yet to be encountered, that night so eventful for my drowsy luck because I discovered you. I gave up my heart in the thoughts of you just then and there itself pleading my luck to let me stay with you all cozied up for not just that night but all nights written in my life.

LOVE STRIKES AT RANDOM

You can not escape the wrath of love, it follows you everywhere till your grave and strikes at random, at any instant like a drizzle of rain in the hot sunny summer afternoon out of the blue. Love is what I'd describe as necessary evil to survive the complicity of this domestic world that we thrive in, but it comes with its own set of repercussions as it has certainly for ages. The pain of heart breaking into gazillion little pieces whilst it actually lays right behind the hollow cavities of your chest, as if your soul has been drenched of all its happiness and you have been stabbed with a gust of lonely, melancholic evenings, nights and mornings basically in continuation of your sorrows till you find the antidote to this everlasting state of gloom. However when it's really down to the time, your time finally of finding the one just the right one who can heal the wounds of long back inscribed on your body like the marks borne by warriors post battle, the cavity in your chest feels no longer empty, hollow or deprived of exhilaration and jubilation. It's instead occupied by the once broken heart in all its senses, right back there reinstated in all its glory.

LOVE ON ROADS

The roads have often taken me to places where I've never intended to be in but nevertheless for the sake of reaching somewhere you've to give up the angst against the roads because these muddy, gravel laden, city or countryside roads be it any they're your only source of either making it big, reaching somewhere finding the joys of life, liberty and love or else like a descending ladder you could reach the bottom of the pit and maybe never come out of that bubble. The secret my friend is to admire whatever may come your way: the people, their lives and even the livestocks they're in possession of. Sometimes you come across eye charming beauties of the land waiting for their perfect suitors idly spending their time in a family cultured environment just shyly peeping from jagged windows with screen slightly opened just as to let some sunlight in but also to have a quick glance over, the man from the city. You wish you could pronounce your love, evidently at first sight for someone, anyone to be precise so you could just spend the nights in someone's arms rather than on stocks of hay piled up for grazing goats all alone under the majestic beauty of night.

TREACHERY OF JUSTICE

Many a nights have passed while I did nothing but sat under the warmth of the oil lamps, bugged by buzzards in the dark. Solitude my only companion, the silence my peacemaker the night under a thick penchant for someone to love, to adore and appease when you feel the world crumbling, tearing you apart maybe even turning against you but the only thing for sure is that hand you've latched onto won't let you fall into the stream of gators waiting to prey upon you. The world is cruel and its justice so irrelevant the sufferings of the sufferers, heartbroken and others never quenched they live in a perpetual state of despair longing for affection but only gets delivered in all its rage, pompous sadness unloading grief of seven seas washing ashore to the purge of destiny where stars are aligned so to collude with future, nothing but unhappiness befalls you while you look for a companion. Breathing life out of my soul, ink running out and a choked throat I can't express words in any form but yonder over my last words, keep looking for love.

HOPE YOU REMEMBER

I've walked many miles for you my love in the rising sun of the morning till its dark and you could see no more of the roads drenched in perspiration, my heart beating twice its capacity. I kept looking around the insipid neighborhood for a quick glance of yours, the smell of yours or maybe those doe like glittery eyes of yours. How I've missed those chats in the park around the bushes amidst all chaos but my sole attention transfixed on you and your words jumbling mid sentence jumping ships from one story to another constantly gazing into my eyes and mine into yours whilst you tapped my shoulders to check if I've not passed out looking into those ocean deep eyes. Now here we are, haven't been in touch for a year, been walking and looking for where those steps of yours trodden along mine and arms wrapped mine but now I can feel the vacuum filled with emptiness and grief still I'll keep walking looking for you, hope you remember me too.

Temptations Of The Heart

The pulsating beats of her heart brushing past my chest like shockwaves, bemusing my petty ears the cackles of her laughing face up so close the wiring in my head went all berserk for I could feel the hapless despair of a sailor stranded in the ocean on a raft watched upon by the seagulls of crowd to them I was a mad man staring into the ways of her joyous life but my life was pledged to her etched on every muscle of my body the undying vow of love smeared in blood. I knew the moment I heard the beats of her anklets in synchrony of the setting sun that I was drenched in the sea of love, the gold bead like sweat trickling down her forehead which if permitted by God to stop the time in motion I'd collect in the jars of my memory the memory of the aroma of her soul, memory of her callous laughter jumping around peers unaware of my unfateful existence. I smiled away, away and away from the only living existence of the visual magnanimity of my life, my transient humane life.

LOVE SEEPS ITS WAY

When I look back over the diary of my memories filled with thoughts of the years I've spent fooling around looking for love in places where there was nothing but a petty heartbreak at every street and every corner. Some nights I wondered if the stars were aligned so in my fate that I had to bear the weight of being unworthy for love. Through ups and downs and the patches of relationships a tremulous grief set across my heart that made my breath heavy, voice flat and eyes teary but I kept looking on. The purpose of life is to spend days in service of the society but one needs companionship, that warmth which is infused by love. To loosen up after a long arduous day someone to care for, to look out for but most importantly to love for. As I remembered my struggles I came across the revelation that I had not thought of all this for a long time now because I had found the one to live and love for. I remember now only the sweet memory of hers and how I spend my days and nights in the thoughts of someone I trust so I live on in her memory.

LOCKS OF LOVE

Of the many contraptions of life, the silliest and loveliest one is that of love. All your life no matter how hard you try to get away from it or even try to run as fast as possible it catches you. The symptoms are even more trickier than your regular illnesses and extremely contagious too. You get lost in the world of daydreams, losing all sense of prudence doing irrelevant stuff completely unaware but what's most striking is the smile, yes the smile that's permanent like it has been glued onto your face whenever you think of this contraption. It pulls you into the depths of almost lovesanity, well that's what I'd call it very close to love but little away from insanity. You become someone you are actually not, start tuning in with the likes and dislikes of your partner. The world is not your go to place anymore rather the four walls with someone you've tremendous affection for. You're trapped happily in the   locks   of   love.

LOVE-A FASHION STATEMENT

If love is a fashion statement wear it, wrap it right around the heart. It's not something to indulge in just for the sake of an experience, to flaunt and wear your heart at the sleeves. It's something you live for, the fashion of love will shield you, adore you once you've got the right taste of it. You don't go around throwing hoops over people, choosing them as per your convenience and ending it when you've derived all your pleasure out of it. This is the worst, to suck out the happiness from your partner, using them and then just leaving abruptly that's not the definition of being in love. You love someone you stay loyal, committed anything to be decided should be mutual. There must always exist a sense of respect for the other person and enough space to breathe, to have one's own identity. You aren't ought to be defined by who you are with, you have to be you that's a man or woman with a strong character. When you like someone, you work out the difference not leave behind the other all alone in the sinking ship. You take them along, all the way over the cliffs or down the road that's love and that's what you should imply if you correlate fashion with it.

PRIVILEGE OF LOVE

It's one of life's greatest privileges to find love and hold onto someone's hand for a lifetime. To find even if for a brief period the clutches of certainty to retain comfort in someone's heart would be one of life's well remembered virtues. The days of love would make you capable of unraveling the tangled beauties of the world that lay hidden to the eyes of those unloved passersby. To retrieve love that lasts is an arduous task and not many are able to lay seize on someone's heart for long. Even after years of conjugal love in many wedlocks the love merely exists or floats on the surface, there's no depth. To sing verses of love, adorning with flowers your beloved and performing other such acts could be elements of love which I won't deny but the ones that matters is how you care for someone in sickness, when they're down and all low grasped by loneliness. What's that love which only exists for visual retreat. I ask from you not the elite flowers of gardens most beautiful but comfort in alms of your love where seclusion for years feels like just a moment of passion that passed in the snap offingers.

ETERNAL ATTACHMENT

I've left behind the golden roads of love somewhere down the years back in memory. I still remember though you illuminating the gloomy and messy evenings of mine with your chirpy voice and charming smile. There was some magical melody in her voice for she seemed to put me in a trance of love. I chased for you in the streets of love following the smell of her soul, through every street there must be none that I must have left. You came through the windows of my life like a force of wind, when it was nothing but a drought, devoid of emotions. However with your love you helped me rediscover my languid self devastated by years of pain that I don't even remember how they got here in the first place. You led me into your palace of hope, mesmerizing with your affection for everything that had life. I won't deny there was a change in me caused by the aura of yours, just by being in your circle I discovered how I had been wrongly conceiving life to be a playground of miseries but I was wrong. You not just won me over but won over every drawback that lay within the depths of my soul for which I'd be eternally grateful to yourlove.

GETTING ON WITH LOVE

How you have broken my heart into terribly tiny pieces, like shards of glass. You've robbed me of my love on transient dark nights when I used to break into verses of love. Now what I've got left over is shrieks of sorrow and loss of words. The verses are incomplete without you and your essence blossoming in the bosoms of corner where once my heart used to lay on the beds of roses caressed by your tender touch and soulful jest. We lived a life of our own in love unaware of what people cared for, I still remember the days of merciless defence that I alone set up for your sake behind the garrison of my love like the sea never ceasing to stop and strong as a boulder which words couldn't pierce. Now that you're not a part of this messy struggle of love, I'm running all alone to a diametrically opposite world of the broken in an infinite circle of life confused as if suddenly I've been set out of my cage into a dark labyrinth getting out of which has become increasingly difficult without your hand on my shoulder pacifying me when I used to lose myself among the people. You helped me stand up and maybe I'll remember those very words of encouragement to get over you.

NEED YOU

No I won't ask for your love. I've earned it in my heart by pledging myself to your heart. I'll wait till time comes asking me to leave my mortal flesh into heaven or hell, I'll keep on loving you till I've my memory of you. Your thoughts are enclosed in the shrines of my heart where erasing you isn't a possibility, whatsoever not even a reality. I've etched you, imprinted you forever in the canvas of my memory, I'll keep thinking of you when I breathe or if I sleep. These trees sway like your hair and winds move like you do, swift as a bird flying into the infinite sky. You'll live on in these words and ink of mine for the posterity to remember. My heart cries your name when this world tries to distance us from ourselves. There's this increasing need of yours to survive, you've got me high on you that even if I try to hide what I feel for you it isn't a possibility. You're to be mine even if its all in my mind. There's only a single throne in my heart that will be forever yours or else vacant in nostalgia. You may feel I've been a pit in your path but there's nothing I won't do for you, your love and the opportunity to find a place in yourheart.

TASTES OF LOVE

I could love you in a thousand different ways, just in case you wake up someday with a feeling, sensation or tingling that you somehow consider an omen of not loving me, maybe you feel bored of me. I can promise you into believing that your senses and omens have failed you miserably. I know that I'm a terrible lover but my love for you is true and this I can say with pride, 'No one can love you like I do'. I could come under your windows with a bunch of flowers, from your favorite gardens of different colours that will make your day brighter than it already is as you discover the depths of my love. Let me take you to the beaches where I can hold you while the breeze sways your hair and I get the pleasure of being so close to you, breathing with you. I can look into your eyes and feel many emotions rushing through my heart but I just keep looking and smiling at your face. My loss of words is symbolic of my tremendous love foryou.

LOVE FOR NIGHTS

The late winter's night as I sat across the room eyes transfixed gazing into the blemishes of sky filled with a blanket of dazzling diamond like minute entities conspiring to let bystanders lose time in awe of their glory and beauty. I too one of these looked into their games of forming random shapes or constellations as you may have rightly guessed imprinted in the dark pitch blackc like one of Van Gogh's paintings. The night to me appears like his last painting for sure before he suffered traumatically to his grave but I'm in awestruck of this night and not in shambles mourning an unfateful death. Amongst all these stars there was the everlasting star of the late night show hidden behind the childish nonchalant clouds preying upon the old hound unaware of its mighty old existence. The never stopping clouds young, ruthless and filled with lust for life moving frantically around the aged but surprisingly undull moon. The actual king of the night who has stood his ground, thumping upon the twinkling stars. It's serene light guiding the souls through lost nights. Oh! How I'd relish the opportunity to sail my night through the luscious sea of stars to my moonland. Far far away from the commotion, the madness that runs intricately in our lives that we've become complacent captives of our motives that we can't differ the living from the dead. What are we then 'The Living Dead?' running behind money, power and holdings. Have we thought of the adrenaline rush of the exhuming flare of our youthful days in admiration of some bitter love story which we relinquished with utmost difficulty leaving us broken or remembering those chirpy minutes with friends for old time's sake spending time with people who mattered. We've forgotten to live. To enjoy is to live. To fulfil dreams is to live. To admire the beautiful is to live. I'm living when I'm musing in awe of the moon and its pals the dazzling stars. The boats empty, no commuters wandering are these clouds in search of souls waiting to drop them in moonland. All interspersed in letting us live few moments to lie back in some distant land, on the mountain top bareback and barefoot on soft grass breathing fresh gust of sea wind gazing into the moonlit sky. The damp soil touching my soul not skin. My putrified heart and soul blended into one for few moments when I let my aspersionsn take control of me, I exhumed with all due exuberance the thoughts that latched onto me and returned my days of chirpy childishness infront of my dazy eyes like a dream I know in the subconscious if I wanted to I could wake up but no I lived it all again in mere few seconds. Those days of living shall remain etched in my memory and I headed back for the dead and deserted town of the living dead. The living dead my present my future into continuum until then cloud my wayfarer, the stars my bridge and the moon my destination.

LOVE FOR BEACHSIDE

Somedays I wish to sit facing the sea maybe lie back on the soft sands gazing, funny shapes these clouds make in the sky all while the sun watches over like some paternal head of the family its children from above with some sense of responsibility, a towering figure. Meanwhile I doze off in peace for few minutes of course as the water from the sea tickles my feet sending shivers and chills of all sorts across my spine and viscera. Every tiny bit of hair on my arm standing up in defiance to this mischief of the water compensating for my tolerance, staring down like an army of Romans. You see this non connection between my mind and body, the disconnection between what I feel and what I do needs to be pacified like a toddler who keeps pulling on his mother pestering for candies. My thoughts pester my body, maybe the cool breeze of the approaching evening moving to and fro can sing me to sleep with a lullaby just for me that sounds just like one of those Beethoven melodies as if he's playing for me. Perhaps his soul has come back in the form of these winds whispering my name in my ears for the only audience he's got to perform for. As I descend to sleep so does the sun, the majestic figure drenched in saffron of the evening sky and not pinching sunstrokes but strokes of love fondling my hair bidding adieu receding into the dark night. The pristine moon, the stars and the ever constant breeze take over cajoling me while I sleep abandoning my thoughts. I've become one with time, lost in between what's real and not any moment I could step into my dream and wake up in some other world leaving my tempestuous life behind. It wouldn't have been just a dream or possibility but a stark reality if it hadn't been for the waters of the sea trickling down just over my knees now. I woke up with these beautiful celestial bodies wrapped overhead facing me telling it's time I wake up, the breeze still whispering but now asking me to move on and I must walk back on the cool sands beside the waters to home, to where I belong.

LOST ON ROADS

I have been walking down these roads for a time long enough now waiting morbidly for someone or something to accompany me in the pinpricks of this world. I feel lonely enough while sitting by the roads again doing nothing but indulging in the game of hope for somebody to show up across me magically carrying me to my destination. The afternoon sun pricking like thorns of the desert and the night so chilly that gives you frost bites of Alaska. Here I'm in this time trying my luck but nothing comes off it. I just keep sitting wandering if I made the right choices. What could become of me if I had been on a different journey with people that tried earlier to stop me. But I don't regret this opportunity traveling down south when the winds offered me to carry in its motherly lap to up north. I refused humbly walked past luxuries denying myself the privilege of enjoying glory. I walked and walked tirelessly like some sage in search of the doors to heaven. Becoming somewhat close to one city haggard myself. No I don't need the sympathies for I'm no destitute but another wanderer unsatisfied looking for love over pleasures. At the end I've traveled far to lands I've never seen before but found very little of what I'd hoped for. But would I stop? No no shrill cries came within me and I set off again on the fiery tracks bound southside.

BACKDOORS OF HEART

Would you let me inback,
Through the doors of your,
Memories into the dreams,
That you rule that you are,
In control for maybe just,
Maybe I could find myself,
A little space in the cruel,
World by the shore with,
You cherishing the green,
Grass blue skies and clear,
Sea laying infront of us the,
World outside your dreams,
A small home filled with,
giggles and serenity.

Oh! What a pity that it,

Couldn't be a reality not,

Ever not now for you don't,

Sleep often at nights and,

I can't stand facing you on,

Mornings that sullen face,

Eyes sunk deep the doe like,

Gait disappearing into the,

Corners of non ephemeral,

Cortex where everything,

Grinds into a revengeful,

Hate waiting and brewing to,

Explode all over my dismal,

Mere existence and now my,

Dream to live in yours is a,

Distant burning effigy.

FAITH IN SEASON PERFECTION

Look out the window ofyour,
Eyes as far as you wish to go,
Beyond push yourself limits,
Let bonkers over opportunities,
Run wild with arms wide in air,
Free yourself your mind clear,
The clutter for you're more than,
Thee think you are forget what,
Says the world it's season of,
Perfection of faith in perfection,
Strive for love you deserve make,
A name that stands out amongst,
All of us believe in thyself world's,
A small place find what amazes,

You makes you sleep less at night,

Run more on days this season is,

Of cold opinions blunt like crystal,

Snow and warm response blossom,

Of ideas outpouring of creative,

Insights perfection is a season,

Across all bays lands over the,

Seven seas as well those seeking,

Faith in perfection taste its delightful,

Beauty not it's bound by months,

Or nature it's bound by grit in your,

Heart and temperament of mind,

Think beyond possibilities of this,

World people might stab questions,

On your back remember as I say,

The faith is perfection not all,

Withstand its discovery your voyage,

To its search an amusing journey,

Not known of but it's your time and,

You own it live up to your life because,

Haven't   got   you   a   pair   of   it.

Let Me Be

Let me be in thisworld,
Filled with sufferings,
Some crippled's staff,
Guiding them away,
From the terrible miseries,
Of life.

Let me be in this world,
Filled with injustice,
Someone's pathfinder,
When they feel lost,
Guiding them to a,
World full of just and cause.

Let me be in this world,
Filled with pain,
Someone's beloved,
Giving them the love,
So desperately they seek,
Washing away all memories of agony.

Let me be in this world,
Filled with lies a man,
Of honour and valor,
Fighting for the sufferings,
Of people and searching,
For the eternal truth.

Things You Do For Love

You havingleft,
These sore eyes,
Reflect my pain,
As streaks of tear roll down my chin.
Would I wait as I did for years?
For your love my dear,
Why wouldn't I,
For losing you is my only fear.
Hurt I am,
Coz your love's stinging,
And painful it is,
For heartbreak is real.
Your door's locked,
Number's gone,

Pictures none,

Is this how cruel is your love.

Haunts me my nightmares,

Since you let go of my hand,

And the new guy you're meddling with,

Wish it is actually myth.

Captured you in,

The polaroids of my heart,

You and me together is what I want,

Frivolous I sound but these things,

"You do for love."

First Kiss

How could Iforget,
The night was I closest,
To you feeling your heart,
Loving your soul.
Your eyes filled with tears,
Heart with fears,
Your lips spoke my name,
Love's really not a game.
Sparks flew in the air,
Unsure of where we were,
Touched your tender lips with mine,
With our breaths aligned.
Hearts that beat together,
Beat for each other,

Bodies that can't resist the other,

This is true love I wonder.

Hold me close to you forever,

This distance I want never,

Don't say no to my love ever,

Without you my life's nothing oh dear!

That First Touch

Those tender touches,
Can these be ever forgotten,
I want you more these days,
Wish I could hold you often.
Feel my love,
For I have never been loved,
You're the one that I always,
Dreamt for but been always cheated before.
With pain in my eyes,
And a stitched heart,
I feel you my love,
More than you are destined for.
One of these days,
I might be gone,

But from the gates of heaven,

I will wreak my love.

I will watch you,

I will feel you,

I will be there for you,

Whenever you search for.

Let the world know,

I loved you so hard,

All this began,

By a tinge of your tender touch.

Test Of Love

Your love's mypoison,
For I chose to drink it with passion,
But your love's a thorn,
Hurts even though you're gone.
Will I ever forget your eyes?
Your clumsy quirks,
Your cheesy lines,
And your cold love.
Gorgeous like the rose,
Tender like it's petals,
I wonder why your love's so harsh,
Makes me weep everytime I try to laugh.
Lost my smile,
Broke my heart,

Messed my mind,
All for your love.
Loving you was like a tempest,
Putting my patience up for a test,
But here I am tugged upon my boat,
Venturing out for my love long lost.

Down The Aisle
Behind the days of ourlives,
The nights together we loved,
Tears when you were gone.
Vivid is the image of,
The dawn you acknowledged our love,
Bemused was I when,
You broke my trust.
I want to hold your hand,
And walk back home down the aisle,
Where we sit by the creek,
Kindling our love.

If Heart Could Speak

Are locked in theircells,
Afraid I'm to let go of them,
Worth it's not to lose hold of thee.
Don't let me be alone,
I'm ready to die for your,
Love my sweetheart,
I want thy heart.
My heart will go on,
Miles for your love,
I'll hum whilst waiting for,
Our time to come.
I know my heart sings for,
Your name it beats for,
I feel you every moment,
As your absence stings on.
I hear your voice,
In my dreams,
I want you,
My love to hold on.
You don't know,

What you mean for,

Me and my life,

For you complete me or else would I be none.

I want to grow,

Old with sitting,

In our farm,

Holding your hand.

Stop meddling my heart,

Oh love! it hurts.

Mon Amour

Untouched bylove,
No chance of discovering at first sight,
But I found my soulmate,
When your eyes met mine.
Spare me a corner in your heart,
For I want to build a small world,
Keep me warm there,
Adore me with your love.
Love happens all time,
But the chemistry isn't always right,
You were some hidden story,
Waiting to complete mine.
I guess angels aren't a fantasy,
For I witnessed one in you,

Lost myself countless times,
As I daydream of you.
The sparkle in your eyes,
Glow on the cheeks,
Child inside a heart,
Is there anything I didn't need?
I think of kneeling down,
Holding your hand,
Laying kisses on them,
And pronouncing my love.
Oh lord! Let her be mine,
She's the angel I dreamt of when I was nine,
My life is hers so am I,
Let the world know she's now mine.

What If

What if I tellyou,
I still love you,
The way I did,
When you were gone.
Vivid is still our love,
Illuminating my heart,
As the memories of you,
Bring tides of tears.
I'm stuck on you,
Haven't yet got enough of you,
Come to me,
I'm yet to fill you with my love.
Night long I fight,
With flashes of nightmare,

From the trauma,
Of my sour heartbreak.
How easy it's for,
You to forget the,
Night we first crossed,
Paths and our eyes met.
If I could hold you,
One last time wish,
The world stopped just right there,
For me to get you back.
My life's a mess,
You are my essence,
Your love completes me,
Setting my soul free.

Dream Of False Hopes

Weren't the starsbrighter,
Wasn't the night shorter,
Feels like was I in a dream,
For few last weeks.
Everything felt right,
Unaware was I that,
Nothing lasts forever,
Neither happiness could be mine ever.
Built a castle of dreams,
For you to live in,
Never did I know,
You made it a home of false hopes.
Didn't we dream,
This all together,

Then how come I'm broken,
Whilst you dream for some others.
My heart's a broken window,
My dreams all tainted,
Wish you hadn't painted,
My love all blue.
This my reality,
Where I strive,
Love stories here's a myth,
Where heartbreak's the only truth.
What if this never happened,
What if I had never woken,
Would you have found me?
Surely for love's a game,
And destiny the master.

Last Few Days

Last FewDays,
These nights have been longer,
The pain has been stronger,
Expressed emotions I have earlier,
But this distance has been bothersome.
Testing times are these,
Filled my heart with hopes,
Maybe somebody would stop,
Hold my hand walk me back,
For lost I have the strength to talk.
Set me free let me breathe,
These four walls feel like prison,
Some nights I lay on my bed,
Wishing it could just all end.

This time demands more time to change,

Somebody explain this please to ky heart,

That just wishes to escape,

For these boundaries have left me dented.

Silence around me,

Screams within me,

My mouth's shut,

But my heart speaks too much.

FRAIL LIKE FEATHER

Frail like afeather,

Is my mind so is my heart,

Rips into pieces when we're apart,

Sometimes I feel a part of me lives in you.

When your heart beats,

Feels like it beats for me too,

I shed tears but the,

Pain is all yours.

Sometimes all I need,

Is to hold you tight,

Keep talking all night,

For this night is my foe,

It won't let me sleep and won't let me go.

Lost in some maze I am,

Feels like it's the time of night,

Walking alone on the roads blindfolded I am,

I need you to hold my hand and guide me to the bright days full of light.

For my heart's a dark place,

Filled with years of grief,

And mind's a total mess,

Filled with voids and thoughts like these.

Keep me afloat like this feather,

Help me again to fly high,

I want to be in that blue sky,

Alone not this time though coz I found my happiness in your eyes.

Bug Of Love

This flower reminds me of you,
These evenings hurt me,
As I take trip down,
The memory lanes,
The nights are the toughest,
As I lie sleepless,
Drooling over you,
Your thoughts racing across my mind.
Feels as if time has stopped,
Life's not moving,
Things supposed to aren't happening,
The pain's imminent.
This pain won't leave me soon,
They say it right,

Love's a parasite,
Leaves you soulless.
These flowers fill the void,
Of the emptiness in my life,
As I remember you,
From the last flowers given by you.
Love does hurt,
But it's a beautiful pain,
Lucky are those to,
Have felt it.
Is it love I need,
Or is it you,
Confusing love is at times,
For answers to it is a mystery.

Crossroads Of Heart

I stand at thecrossroads,
You left me at,
With teary eyes,
And heart filled with hopes.
Confused I am,
To trod past which road,
One leads to you,
Other to oblivion.
Shattered myself for you,
Will never reminisce your love,
Filled my heart is with pain that's due,
Feelings of mine have I now shoved.
Will choose the path other,
Of course that leads to not you,

Forgotten will be I,

Long gone be my existence.

Difficult is to move on,

Left I'm with options none,

Leaving you is heart wrenching,

But it's my life that I'm stitching.

These roads may never lead to you,

Never may I even see you,

Your words would though ring my ears,

Will help me get on with my life and,

Live like I did once upon.

www.ingramcontent.com/pod-product-compliance
Lightning Source LLC
LaVergne TN
LVHW050420160726
843469LV00041B/1160